THE SUMMER CAT

Story and Pictures by Howard Knotts

Harper & Row, Publishers

Knotts

Library of Congress Cataloging in Publication Data
Knotts, Howard.
The summer cat.

SUMMARY: A small boy comes to accept that he can't
keep a cat he loves when it belongs to someone else.
[1. Cats—Fiction] I. Title.
PZ7.K7615Su 1981   [E]   79-9610
ISBN 0-06-023178-5
ISBN 0-06-023179-3 (lib. bdg.)

FOR ANNIE AND BEN CHENEY

Annie and Ben ran and ran. The light was leaving the evening sky and fireflies flickered here and there in the dark places under the bushes. Down to the meadow and back they ran, and Sloppy, their dog, ran with them. Out of breath at last, they sank down in the still-warm grass and looked up at the sky through the apple tree leaves.

It was then they first saw the calico cat.

"She's beautiful," Ben whispered.

The cat was perched in the apple tree. It was small, not a kitten, but not full grown either.

"Look at her colors!" Annie exclaimed.

"He's white and orange and black and yellow and red," said Ben.

"He's a *she*," said Annie. "Calicos are *always* girls."

The little cat glowed like a strange, wonderful flower in the fading evening light. Even Sloppy seemed under her spell.

"I'm going to call her Apple Blossom," Ben said.

As it got darker they tried to coax the calico down, but she wouldn't budge. So Annie and Ben put out milk and scraps for the cat, and they took Sloppy to bed with them so he wouldn't eat her food. From their bedroom window they watched the apple tree.

"She couldn't have come from the cornfield," said Ben.

"She must have come from the meadow," said Annie.

"Wherever she came from," said Ben, "I hope she's come to stay."

In the morning the calico cat was gone.

"I'll find her," Ben said, and off he went into the tall meadow grass. Annie could hear him calling from far away. He was hot and tired when he came home for lunch.

"I looked and looked," he said, "all the way up to the edge of the woods. She isn't anywhere."

But that evening the meadow grass parted and out came the calico cat. Sloppy ran to meet her, followed her across the lawn, and watched as she climbed up the apple tree.

"Where *was* she?" asked Ben, scratching his head.

"She was probably sleeping all day someplace in the meadow," said Annie.

They talked to the cat in cooing voices. Slowly she came down to a lower branch and let herself be petted.

"Listen to her purr," Ben said. "Have you come to stay, Apple Blossom?"

The next morning the cat was gone again—only to return that evening.

Ben was bewildered. "Where does she go when she's gone?" he kept asking.

The next evening she came to them right away and let them scratch her head. Then she and Sloppy ran back and forth across the grass until finally she bounced up the apple tree. Sloppy settled himself underneath.

"She still has enough kitten in her not to be afraid of dogs," said Annie.

"She knows *he* wouldn't hurt her," said Ben.

When it was nearly dark, they went inside the house for milk and scraps. Sloppy had a lost look about him when they came out again. The calico cat had disappeared.

"Oh, Apple Blossom," said Ben, "I wish I knew where you went."

It was the same the next day and all the days that followed. Every evening Apple Blossom would come out of the thick meadow grass. Sometimes she stayed late. Sometimes she left

early. But even if she stayed till the stars were out and the moon was high and Annie and Ben were in their beds, she was always gone in the morning.

Once they took her up to bed. For a while she seemed content, but then she paced the room and meowed in such an unhappy way, they had to let her out.

"You can't keep Apple Blossom where she doesn't want to be," said Ben, shaking his head.

Every evening she came. She came for their cookouts. She came for Ben's birthday.

"She's the most mysterious cat," Ben said, giving her a piece of his cake, "and I love her."

The others loved her too, but it was Ben who loved her most.

All summer long she came—except on rainy days.

"Where do you think she goes on rainy days?" Ben wanted to know, and Annie shrugged. "Someday," said Ben, "I'll find out."

Sometimes Apple Blossom went running and rolling with Sloppy, and if he played too rough, she would swipe his nose with her paw. Sometimes they sat together. Sometimes they washed each other. And sometimes they fell asleep together, all curled up in a heap.

Before long it was late summer. The apples had gotten bigger and were beginning to turn red. When Apple Blossom sat among them in the tree, she seemed more beautiful than ever.

"See how big she's gotten," said Ben one night. "Now she's a full-grown cat."

One morning Annie and Ben woke up to gray skies and a dripping rain.

After breakfast Ben packed his raincoat pockets with a peanut butter sandwich, three pickles, two hard-boiled eggs, an apple, some oatmeal cookies, and a screw-top soda bottle filled with water. "I won't be home for lunch," he explained.

When he got back late in the afternoon, his face was sad.

"What's the matter?" Annie asked.

"Apple Blossom has a home. She belongs to the summer lady who stays in that blue house on the other side of the woods."

"You mean Apple Blossom goes all that way?" said Annie.

"She *lives* there," said Ben. "She sat right in that lady's lap. I watched them. She just comes over here to visit."

Annie could tell Ben was close to tears. "Ben," she said slowly, "didn't you ever think Apple Blossom just might have a home?"

"No," said Ben. "I thought she lived somewhere in the meadow and would come to us when it got cold outside. Now she'll leave with that lady."

Apple Blossom returned the evening after the rain. Ben stroked her and talked to her in his softest voice.

"I'm going to make her love me more than that summer lady," he told Annie. "Then she'll stay here."

"Ben, that's mean," said Annie. "The summer lady probably loves her just as much as you do."

"She *couldn't*," said Ben, "and anyway I don't care how mean I am."

The evenings came early now. The summer was nearly done.
One dark afternoon a different kind of rain came sweeping
across the meadow. It was a cold, pounding rain that lasted two
days. On the evening of the third day the sky cleared and there
was the smell of fall in the air as the trees let go of their leaves.

This time Apple Blossom didn't come back.

Annie watched Ben's face. "I guess maybe she's gone for good now," she said softly. "It had to happen."

"Guess so," said Ben. He stood with his hands in his pockets looking at the ground.

"Are you all right, Ben?"

"Don't worry," said Ben, "I'm tough."

On the morning of the fourth day Annie and Ben saw a plump, gray-haired woman standing with their mother on the front porch.

"That's the summer lady," Ben whispered.

"It's about that beautiful calico cat," their mother said. "She hasn't been home for four days. Have you seen her?"

Annie and Ben shook their heads. The summer lady looked very sad. They could tell she had been crying because her eyes were red.

"We'll look for her," Annie said.

When the summer lady left, their mother said, "That poor woman is brokenhearted. She needs that cat. You two look hard." Then she went into the house.

"If Apple Blossom isn't there and she isn't here," Annie said, "something must have happened to her."

Ben shrugged. "She's just gone."

"For a person who loves her so much you don't seem to be too worried."

"I'm tough," Ben said.

Annie looked at Ben a long time. "Ben," she said finally, "where is she?"

"Who?"

"Apple Blossom."

"I don't know."

"Ben, you're lying. Where is Apple Blossom?"

Ben couldn't look at Annie. "Well," he said in a low voice, "I've got her in the back of the basement. She's locked in the old root cellar."

"Ben, that's terrible. How long have you had her there?"

"Since before the rain. I've been feeding her good. She's my cat."

"She's not your cat," said Annie. "We have to take her back."

"She's mine," said Ben. "I named her and I love her the most."

"That doesn't make her your cat," Annie said. "You know you can't keep her in that root cellar forever."

Ben was biting his lip. "She hates it in there," he whispered.

"Then we'd better get her out while Mom's upstairs," Annie said gently.

When they took Apple Blossom out into the sunshine and put
her down at the edge of the meadow, she rubbed against Ben's
leg.

"She doesn't seem mad at me," Ben said.

"She's just glad to be free, you dumb dope," said Annie.

24

Apple Blossom turned and went into the meadow. Annie and Ben followed. Sloppy was close behind. When they came out of the woods, Apple Blossom ran toward the blue house.

The summer lady was sitting in the yard. When Apple Blossom jumped in her lap, she held her close and kissed her. She didn't seem able to speak right away.

"She showed up after you left," said Annie.

"Her name is Apple Blossom," said Ben in a choked voice.

"Yes, your mother told me," said the summer lady. "I've been calling her Cat, but now I'm going to call her Apple Blossom, too. The name just suits her." She thanked them again and again and wanted to hear all about Apple Blossom's evening visits. She invited them inside her house.

Annie said they couldn't stay. "Mom wants us home right away," she said. Annie could see how hard Ben was trying not to cry.

She and Ben said good-by to Apple Blossom and turned and walked toward the woods.

Once inside the woods Ben couldn't keep his tears back any longer. Annie put her arm around his shoulders.

"I'm not afraid to cry if I love something," Ben said.

"I know," said Annie. She felt tears in her own eyes.

"That red-eyed summer lady would cry worse than me," said Ben. "Without Apple Blossom, she would cry her brains out. We had to give her back."

"Yes," said Annie, "we had to give her back."

"That lady would have cried like Niagara Falls. I probably saved her from drowning," said Ben, wiping his eyes.

Annie gave Ben a squeeze. She knew that giving up Apple Blossom was the hardest thing he had ever had to do.

"Ben, I like you," said Annie. "You're tough. And you're brave, too."

One snowy November day Annie and Ben were walking
home from school. Ben was very quiet.

"You still miss her?" said Annie.

"I think about her a lot," Ben said.

"She's a summer cat," said Annie. "She belongs to a summer lady and she's just an old summer cat. She'll be back next summer."

Ben sighed and said, "Yes, next summer."

31

And in a window of a tall building in a city far away sat Apple
Blossom looking out at the falling snow. She loved the summer
lady, but she couldn't help dreaming of warm days and the smell
of grass, an apple tree, and two children and a dog named
Sloppy.

YES, NEXT SUMMER.

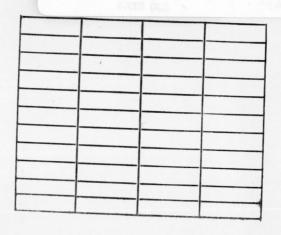

81
82   83   84   85   86   07(27)   17(30)
                        18(33)
MAR 24 1981   95
86   91